PRAISE FOR M. L. BUCHMAN

Top 10 Romance of 2012, 2015, and 2016.

— BOOKLIST: THE NIGHT IS MINE,
HOT POINT, HEART STRIKE

One of our favorite authors.

— RT BOOK REVIEWS

Buchman has catapulted his way to the top tier of my favorite authors.

— FRESH FICTION

A favorite author of mine. I'll read anything that carries his name, no questions asked. Meet your new favorite author!

— THE SASSY BOOKSTER, FLASH OF
FIRE

M.L. Buchman is guaranteed to get me lost in a good story.

— THE READING CAFE, WAY OF THE
WARRIOR: NSDQ

I love Buchman's writing. His vivid descriptions bring everything to life in an unforgettable way.

— PURE JONEL, HOT POINT

DILYA'S CHRISTMAS CHALLENGE

A WHITE HOUSE PROTECTION FORCE STORY

M. L. BUCHMAN

Buchman Bookworks

Other works by M. L. Buchman:

The Night Stalkers
MAIN FLIGHT
The Night Is Mine
I Own the Dawn
Wait Until Dark
Take Over at Midnight
Light Up the Night
Bring On the Dusk
By Break of Day
WHITE HOUSE HOLIDAY
Daniel's Christmas
Frank's Independence Day
Peter's Christmas
Zachary's Christmas
Roy's Independence Day
Damien's Christmas
AND THE NAVY
Christmas at Steel Beach
Christmas at Peleliu Cove
5E
Target of the Heart
Target Lock on Love
Target of Mine

Firehawks
MAIN FLIGHT
Pure Heat
Full Blaze
Hot Point
Flash of Fire
Wild Fire
SMOKEJUMPERS
Wildfire at Dawn
Wildfire at Larch Creek
Wildfire on the Skagit

Delta Force
Target Engaged
Heart Strike
Wild Justice

White House Protection Force
Off the Leash
On Your Mark
In the Weeds

Where Dreams
Where Dreams are Born
Where Dreams Reside
Where Dreams Are of Christmas
Where Dreams Unfold
Where Dreams Are Written

Eagle Cove
Return to Eagle Cove
Recipe for Eagle Cove
Longing for Eagle Cove
Keepsake for Eagle Cove

Henderson's Ranch
Nathan's Big Sky
Big Sky, Loyal Heart

Love Abroad
Heart of the Cotswolds: England
Path of Love: Cinque Terre, Italy

Dead Chef Thrillers
Swap Out!
One Chef!
Two Chef!

Deities Anonymous
Cookbook from Hell: Reheated
Saviors 101

SF/F Titles
The Nara Reaction
Monk's Maze
the Me and Elsie Chronicles

Strategies for Success (NF)
Managing Your Inner Artist/Writer
Estate Planning for Authors

---

*M*iss Watson had considered painting a giant spider web on her door. If it wouldn't draw undue attention, she well might have. Room 043-Mechanical in the White House Residence's lowest subbasement had nothing mechanical in it, at least nothing that a building engineer would ever care about. Good cover because the best cover was a bland one.

Her small desk had once belonged to Assistant Secretary of the Treasury, Harry Dexter White, who had run the Silvermaster spy ring for the Soviet Union for years. Her walls were packed with every biography or interview transcript from a spy going back to the early days of the American colonies. The rubbish about The Craft that consumed so much of the CIA's libraries—written by analysts and others even less informed—were not to be found within her four walls. She also kept a number of the more gruesome tools of the trade on display to remind her of just what horrors the human psyche was capable.

But even at her age, a woman wasn't supposed to feel like Moriarty—Sherlock Holmes' greatest opponent —curled "motionless, like a spider in the centre of its web, but that web has a thousand radiations, and he knows well every quiver of each of them."

She rarely left her office anymore, instead listening only to the information that flowed into her domain rather than gathering it. She allowed only a few bits, a very precious few, to flow back out. Maybe she'd paint the spider web in blacklight or some other ink that wouldn't show. But she'd know was there.

It always surprised her when a thread was activated that she hadn't anticipated. When the computer beeped she dropped a stitch in her knitting in surprise—a nice bit of double-sided colorwork scarf recalling a long ago sunset along the shore of the Black Sea.

Assumptions are dangerous, she reminded herself.

She forced herself to pick up the stitch and count to make sure that everything was put to rights before she answered.

"Hello, my dear." Her screen lit to reveal one of her favorite people. Major Emily Beale (retired—at least according to most official records) had a mind that worked so differently from her own. For that reason if no other, Emily would have been very useful to her. But as a force of nature in her own right, the immensely skilled and well-connected woman brought far more assets than most could muster.

However, she should have known a call was coming.

It wasn't unusual for Emily to call from her Montana ranch, but it was strange that she herself had no inkling of what the topic might be.

"Hello, Miss Watson. How are you today?"

"Oh, I'm good my dear. Very good. Thank you for asking. Is there something amiss that I'm unaware of?"

"Not likely."

Miss Watson couldn't quite resist smiling at the compliment. "I don't know that you've ever made a social call before."

Emily's grimace communicated a great deal. It wasn't social, which was disappointing. But she saw in how Emily's eyes shifted to the side, beyond the breadth of the screen she'd be using, that Emily wished it had been. She was such a sweet woman.

"Emily, dear child…" Miss Watson merely said it to herself, but saw Emily react much more strongly than expected.

A laugh?

A hysterical one?

Major Emily Beale was not the sort given to hysterics.

"Tell me the reason you called, then we can talk about why you should have called earlier."

Emily nodded, "I'm worried about Dilya. She keeps placing herself at risk. I don't want her to create a situation that's over her head when she's too young to know what she's doing."

"That child was never young. Such potential." She regretted the last as soon as she said it aloud. She could see the sudden wariness in Emily's eyes—so protective of the teen, despite the girl being adopted not by her but by one of her teammates. That protectiveness was one of Emily's great strengths. Her own instincts were far more honed to self-preservation.

Dilya, as a seventeen-year-old war orphan, was much the same. She'd been afforded the best training imaginable: her deep involvement with the fighting elements of the Night Stalkers 5th Battalion D Company, who had rescued her originally. Her placement in the White House as a nanny and then the dog minder for the First Dog had placed her in the way of exceptional information. Her skills at passing through a room unremarked were truly exceptional. It definitely reminded Miss Watson of her own, long ago youth.

And most importantly, Dilya possessed the sharp mind to go with it.

That girl's mind… Yet Emily had a point.

"The girl is so independent. Perhaps too much so." How different would her own past be if she had learned to rely upon others? Even occasionally?

"Too much?" And there was Emily's limitation. Her definition of success was the survival of her team and the destruction of her target. She was terribly linear. Independence was a lesson that Emily only thought she had learned. She had been embedded in teams her entire life.

"Yes. She knows a great deal more about depending solely on her own judgment than even you, my dear child. Despite your deservedly decorated career. And don't we both know about some of the decorations you can never admit to."

Emily's bland expression would be a sufficient denial —to anyone who hadn't spent a lifetime surviving by studying human body language. She almost considered pointing out how easy she was to read for a professional, but decided that there were some things Emily would be happier never knowing.

Dilya's strength was in her covert gathering of knowledge. But oh, the price that was paid for such a gift. Miss Watson both envied and pitied the girl.

"Dilya has carefully positioned herself to know more than everyone around her," Miss Watson continued, more to herself than Emily. "I even hold a hope that someday she—"

Not yet. She didn't dare think that far ahead. Hope often hurt as much as it helped.

"Well, never mind that now. I believe that you've raised a valid question and I shall give it some thought. It is Christmas soon. Perhaps I shall give her a Christmas gift."

Emily looked relieved to hand off the problem. Miss Watson found that trust to be the nicest compliment of all, it actually warmed her old heart.

"Now, my dear. Let's talk about what's troubling you."

Through the rest of the conversation, Miss Watson wondered at how curiously innocent Emily was. She was one of the finest warriors Miss Watson had ever met, yet she was curiously unaware of what it meant to be a woman.

One thing Miss Watson envied her was motherhood. She herself had launched a hundred women on their careers in espionage, giving birth to their nascent dreams of adventure, danger, and intrigue. But she'd only given her own heart once—and the price that the Cold War had exacted upon her for that single mistake had been a chilly one indeed.

"No woman as beautiful as you with two lovely children and such an exceptional husband can doubt that she is in the prime of her life," she assured Emily.

There was so much she herself had lost.

Lieutenant General Sergei Kulakov of Soviet Union's KGB First Directorate had unwittingly taught the United States more about the Soviet intelligence operations than any other man. As his mistress, she had siphoned away his secrets until it destroyed his life. Like a Stalinesque purge, he and his family were erased from history by the Soviet regime—from re-doctored photos to a "training accident" that had leveled his Black Sea dacha with a firebomb. To this day she didn't know where the leak had come that destroyed her best source and the love of her life in a single, vicious stroke. Whereas Emily…

"And I must compliment you on the fine job you did helping your husband transition to retired life. You are much better with people than you think you are. You picture yourself so austere and remote, yet people are drawn to you anyway." The pain swelled in her chest until she feared it really would kill her. As they had never been drawn to her. Except for that one time. There had never been a man for her like Sergei. "I remember such a time of reflection shortly before I died."

"You…died?"

"Oh yes, dear. Any number of times," Miss Watson shook off the memories. She was the reason they had bombed the dacha, to kill Sergei's mistress. Some instinct had sent her racing away across the Black Sea in a tiny open boat that stormy December night. That instinct had saved her life, if not her heart. She nudged her tiny Christmas tree on the desk, so bright and cheery—it didn't fully mask that old memory, but it helped. It was impossible to look at it without smiling.

"It is an easy way to cover your tracks in an on-going CIA operation. But I'm referring to when I let the CIA itself believe I had died." Because she desperately needed to stop thinking about her cherished Sergei.

"How did they take it?"

"Oh, it was a lovely funeral. I have a star up on their wall, which is quite an honor in my business."

"And they still don't know about you surviving?"

Not a chance. She'd die for real before she'd work for the cretins now in charge. The CIA was no longer about national security or even trade security. It was all about political gain, which she had no stomach for.

"There comes a time in a woman's life where one must move closer to the heart. We aren't men, after all. You'll want to think about that, child. You are a woman grown. You've fought for the right, and done the duties that a man does. For great achievers like us, struggling within a society not ready for us, we must now come to terms with being…ourselves."

"How did you do it?"

She'd been babbling. Now, having professed her

evolved state, she certainly couldn't admit to lacking such. Instead she offered her best enigmatic smile.

"Oh, I became *your* weapon," Emily had thankfully jumped topics. Perhaps her thoughts were more creative than Miss Watson had previously given her credit for. "All those additional black-in-black ops. The toughest missions—"

"—Came to you because of your supreme confidence and exceptional abilities." Oh how she wished she could take credit for Emily's achievements, they were so very impressive. "Don't try to make me the wizard behind the curtain of your career, Emily. You are tactically an exceptional woman. It is the bigger picture that slips by you. Dilya is beginning to see her own bigger picture, which is why you worry about her—we fear what we don't understand."

Yes. Dilya. She was the important one, because she had the potential to be so much more.

"But—"

"Oh, my dear child. In the later years, you are still *yourself*. But the challenges are new. You must learn who you, yourself are. Rediscover or, if that fails, discover for the first time, the amazing woman you are."

"That's your advice?"

"The voice of experience." And perhaps she'd try to follow it someday.

"What did you—"

"Oh no, my dear. It would be cheating to tell," though she might, if she knew. She had grown to like Emily more than any woman in her past. "Besides,

Dilya is far more my daughter than you are—at least in how she thinks. You must discover your own woman."

"Why doesn't that feel helpful?"

"Because you're still thinking as if you live in a man's world, challenging the status quo." And if she didn't help Dilya see that soon, the girl would walk the same horrid path she had. By seventeen, she'd already been recruited and embedded in the depths of the Vietnam War. JFK, such a pretty man, had asked what she could do for her country and she'd joined the CIA. For forty years she'd done the horrific and the unthinkable.

"Miss Watson, are you—"

"It is time I sent for Dilya." She needed to shift the girl's path—immediately. She could only hope she wasn't too late to turn Dilya from the fateful missteps she had made in her own long-ago youth.

"Miss Watson?" Emily sympathy was sweet but misguided.

"Go see your family, dear." She cut the connection and listened.

Not to the noises of the dishwashers flushing water through the pipes that ran along her ceiling. Not the low hum from the massive air conditioning units across the hall. None of her alarms were lit. In fact, at the moment even the laundry and the sub-basement usher's office were unpeopled.

Normally she liked it when she was the only person on this level. At the moment, it left her feeling cold and…old.

ilya had never been called by Miss Watson before. It was a strange experience.

She was in the curator's library on the White House Residence's ground floor. It lay down the hall from the kitchen, between the Secret Service room and the library. When the call came, she'd been poking through the records and trying to find out just how much trouble she was in for letting First Dog Zackie break the small antique table in the hallway outside the First Lady's secretary's office. Especially because she'd supposedly been over in the Residence that morning and not eavesdropping on the second floor of the East Wing.

She'd hoped it was a reproduction and not a 1789 Thomas Sheraton original, but the photo she'd just found in the curator's library wasn't encouraging. It was late at night, so the curator and his assistant had gone home hours ago, not realizing that Dilya had breezed in one door to wave hello and not breezed out the other on her way to the Chocolate Shop as usual. It was one of the advantages of creating predictable patterns, it made other people have assumptions.

Then the assistant curator's phone range.

She'd frozen in place for the three rings, then it stopped.

She knew that voicemail took over at four rings, so she didn't think anything of it…until the senior curator's phone rang three times.

On the third round of ping-pong between the two phones, she gingerly answered one.

There was nothing but silence…and the sound of dishwashers draining through overhead pipes.

All she said was, "Yes, ma'am." before hanging up the phone. The White House was quiet tonight, but she avoided the stairs by the kitchen. Instead, she slipped out the curator office's back door and down the two flights of steps—perhaps the least used in the entire White House. She circled twice around the elevator machinery space and ducked into the lone bathroom at the east end of the lowest subbasement.

Five minutes later, she stepped out. She'd long since observed that most people grew impatient after two minutes. Even most of the Secret Service agents would start looking around by three minutes. By five, almost everyone was bored out of their skull. They'd start moving about, making noise. When she stepped back into the hall, there were only the noises she'd cataloged in her thoughts as "typical" of this level.

Nothing changed as she found her way to Room

043-Mechanical and slipped in through the narrow opening before shutting the door behind her.

"Took your time, girl," Miss Watson sounded almost stern.

"You've never called me before. I decided that I'd better be cautious."

Miss Watson harrumphed thoughtfully. She was never the sort of woman who would grunt, but it seemed to carry meaning—but nothing that Dilya could interpret.

"Have a seat, child."

Dilya used to welcome that diminutive—most people discounted and thus ignored children—but at seventeen, she was finding it less than charming. Especially from someone close to her. But one didn't lightly correct Miss Watson.

She slipped onto the chair and idly wished Zackie was here so that she could scratch his head. He loved her without question or judgment and there were times she needed that. Even her parents would ask about school or boys…as if setting a trap without meaning to.

"What's that?" Dilya bit her tongue, but the little Christmas tree on Miss Watson's desk was very peculiar. Tiny rectangular boxes of red-and-green wire had been stacked up to make a foot-high cone. Miniature blinking lights had been woven through them.

"It's a lobster pot Christmas tree. And, yes girl, sometimes it is best to just ask the question."

It was one of the first things that Miss Watson had ever told her that didn't ring true—there was a strain in her voice as she'd said it. Dilya would have to keep an ear out for why. She also made a note to herself to look up more information about lobster pots. She'd seen lobsters arrive in the kitchen for White House state dinners and knew they'd never fit in these. The entire tree wasn't much bigger than a lobster.

"A gift from a friend."

She'd never thought about Miss Watson having friends, but she supposed everyone did. Of course, everything Miss Watson ever said contained a double or even a triple meaning. *Friend.* Did she herself have them? It was hard to tell. Her world was defined by the adults of the military and the White House, and by the President's and Vice President's newborns who she was a nanny for. Super busy when they were here. Time to observe things when they weren't. Though lately she'd come to appreciate that people observed the baby in a room, but not the person carrying her.

High school had garnered her no friends. The stigma of working personally for the First Family had marked her as an outsider from the beginning, even in the most elite school of Washington, DC. It had also taken her too long to understand that there was such a thing as competitive sports. Her life in war zones had taught her that only victory mattered—only survival. Her intensity didn't go over well in harmless games. She'd learned to temper that instinct, but not soon enough. She'd scared her classmates and they didn't forget that easily.

"That's nice," Dilya finally acknowledged that Miss Watson had friends. It would be nice to have one of her own, who was her own age. But she could count the number of seventeen-year-olds who worked in the White House on one finger. And the number of people who actually lived here on one hand: the three members of the First Family, the rotating watch officer with the Nuclear Football (the launch codes and radio that were never more than a hundred meters from the President), and herself when both her parents were out of town. Which was surprisingly often: her father Archie off consulting and Kee on a training mission, or a live one, with the Hostage Rescue Team.

She didn't mind though, not really. When she slept at the White House, she lived in the same small apartment that Emily Beale had occupied when she'd been a chef here a long time ago. Dilya had seen how good a fighter Major Beale was—even Michael from Delta Force had said the major was especially good. She so wanted to be like her: really smart and totally lethal.

Dilya had hated her looks in her early teens because short girls with Uzbekistani dark skin and riffled hair would never be tall and blonde and bright like Major Beale. Once she'd understood that it wasn't the appearance that mattered, she'd forgiven her heritage and focused on what else she could learn.

"You present a fascinating problem, child."

"I don't mean to." For half an instant she wondered if Miss Watson was referring to the broken Thomas Sheraton table in the East Wing, but decided that was silly. Not that she wouldn't know, but that she wouldn't care. Then Dilya was sorry she presented a problem, because it meant she was doing something imperfectly that must have come to Miss Watson's attention.

"What have you learned in your expeditions today?"

Fridays were generally quiet, especially in the weeks before Christmas. The decorators had been through at the beginning of December and turned the White House into a winter wonderland. How could everyone ooh and ahh over it? It reminded her too much of her freezing walk over the Hindu Kush Mountains of Afghanistan when she'd been a child of ten. She tried not to look too closely in case she imagined her parents' blood spattered on the snow as it had been when they'd been murdered shortly afterward.

Still, she thought of a few things to tell Miss Watson that she heard lately. In the beginning, she wasn't sure if she should share things with the old woman. But then she'd managed to eavesdrop on a surprisingly frank conversation between Miss Watson and Emily Beale regarding the risks of a new White House intern—who was dismissed almost immediately afterward. There were now few things she held back. Because if Emily trusted Miss Watson, so would she—mostly.

Miss Watson nodded in surprise at the passing remark between two of the cabinet secretaries about "coal futures." Yet another thing for Dilya to now research the meaning of the next time she was online.

"Let's have some tea," Miss Watson rose to her feet.

----

3

*D*ilya knew which hidden trigger to press inside the bookcase's shelving to release it so it swing aside.

Miss Watson let her do it herself. The heavy cases were on silent rollers, but they still required force to move—something Dilya did so easily and that she herself now had to work at.

The bookcase folded aside, opening a doorway into her inner parlor. In sharp contrast to the outer library, this was a warm and cozy space. The rich Oriental rug, white-rose wallpaper covered with photos of history's greatest female spies, and the comfortable armchairs before the marble-mantled fireplace was often all that kept her morale up.

She eased into the armchair as Dilya went about making tea and setting out cookies that she herself had baked last night. It was her one solace, a skill she'd learned years ago. She'd learned to cook to endear herself to the men she was spying on, but she'd always baked for herself.

When everything was set out and served, they drank a while in silence. The Harvey and Sons chamomile from Egypt was very floral, but the taste was incredibly smooth and lulled her nerves after even the first few sips.

She looked across at Dilya and tried to think how to teach this girl the lesson that she needed, the lesson that she'd never learned for herself. Yet Emily had done it. How?

Miss Watson had become caught in a trap of her own making. Emily had appeared to take her advice to heart. So, to ask how Emily had learned what Dilya needed—how to value the team above independent action—would have undercut her own advice. It was crucial knowledge, she knew it by her own lack. She'd always undervalued the importance of people in her life as anything other than targets and potential threats.

When Emily accepted the amazing woman she already was, then she would truly step into her power. She hoped that Emily did it soon so that she'd still be alive to watch.

Yet Dilya needed…

"Tell me about your friends."

Dilya's face revealed no telltale expression as Emily's had. Dilya was almost perfectly unreadable. Not chill, but so self-contained that she didn't reveal anything of who she was. It was startling to realize that though she was so pretty, she wasn't beautiful. It was because the girl kept herself locked away so safe behind her mystical green eyes that her features appeared slightly lifeless.

Oh, she could appear animated at a moment's notice, but this blankness was her normal, silent self.

"You have no friends." Miss Watson didn't make it a question.

Dilya didn't argue.

And there was the difference between herself and Emily. Emily had garnered a team, a family, and a circle of friends so loyal that it might take her years to understand their true depths. The only reason that the wives of the White House's leaders—who were so dependent upon Emily—didn't become jealous, was because Emily Beale had won them over as well with her immense integrity. And as the coming years of friendship mellowed the awe they held her in, their true friendships would grow.

Her own friends? All except for a very select group of fellow librarians thought she had died fifteen years ago. And her closest friends might indeed be Emily—who she'd only met once in person—and this young girl watching her so carefully.

That was the different path Dilya must learn to walk.

"I'm sending you to school."

"I already go to school."

"Tomorrow."

"It's the weekend and my high school is closed, but you know that. Which school?"

"The White House kitchen."

Dilya actually let enough emotion through to blink at her in surprise.

"Saturday at nine a.m. And you aren't allowed to leave early."

Miss Watson was very pleased that she was able to finish her tea before Dilya even thought to take another sip of her own.

4

ilya had been in the White House kitchen any number of times, though not nearly as often as visiting Chef Clive in the Chocolate Shop.

Chef Klaus was terribly strict, far more likely to explode with German epithets than to deliver praise. She knew he tolerated her presence, but she'd failed to make him smile even once. He was a tall, spare man, far above her own five-foot five. He seemed to look down at her like a stooping vulture. His tall chef's hat often hanging directly overhead when he was scowling down at her.

This morning, he was in "a mood". She'd heard the pastry chef and soup chef making a joke that if Chef Klaus was ever not in "a mood" the kitchen would freeze over. Only when, three months later, she heard a cabinet member saying he would agree with a new policy when hell froze over, did she understand the chefs' joke. She also knew from listening to the others that he was immensely respected. Whether his kitchen created a plated five-course dinner for two hundred guests or a sandwich for the President to eat in the Oval, the kitchen ran with the same clockwork precision.

He was thumping down bags of flour and sugar. Crashing mixing bowls against one another so hard that she was surprised they didn't break, even if they were steel.

"*Es ist verrückt! Warum heute* must my pastry chef be sick? Someone tell me why?"

"He caught it from his son," Dilya ventured. She liked Chef Emile, who still slipped her choice pastries like she was a little girl. "He brought the cold home from his kindergarten class."

"Eh? Oh, Dilya."

"He must be very sick to not be here, chef."

"So. Today *you* are my assistant?"

"It was…" She didn't think that Chef Klaus would know about Miss Watson. "I heard there was school here today. I thought I'd come learn."

"What? Someone who acts as if I have something to teach them instead of just doing my commands? *Gut! Gut!*" He waved a hand at the pantry. "Bring me butter, five pounds. Molasses, cinnamon, nutmeg, allspice, ginger—crystallized, powdered, and fresh. Well don't stand their looking so surprised. *Schnell! Schnell!* And take them with you." He waved a hand over her shoulder. "Oh, *ja.* Eggs, we must have two dozen to start," he stomped into the walk-in refrigerator to fetch those himself.

"Don't forget the butter while you're in there," she called after him.

"Now she thinks she runs kitchen." At least that's what it sounded like. She didn't know enough German to be certain. She committed it to memory to look up later and see if she was right, *"Jetzt glaubt sie, sie leite die Küche."*

She turned.

Four kids were standing in the doorway, frozen in place as if they'd been cast in ice like the rest of the White House's horrid winter wonderland nightmare.

Everybody in the school knew Trevor, he was captain of the soccer team. He was tall, with dark straight hair and very good-looking. He was standing just a little too close behind Kimberlee. She'd seen Major Henderson do it when he thought his wife needed protecting—as if Major Emily Beale ever needed anyone to do that.

Kimberlee made up for average features with a cheery personality—she was an Alabama senator's daughter with medium skin similar in darkness to Dilya's, but a very different hue. She'd dyed her wavy hair with a blonde so bright it was almost gold. It reminded her of the thin stripe of blonde that her adoptive mother Kee wore in own dark hair, to remember a dead friend. The color choice made her like Kimberlee even if she was one of the school's super-popular crowd.

She didn't really recognize the other two, though she thought she'd seen them around. A tall, serious blonde girl and a boy about her own height with messy brown hair that needed a comb. He was the one scanning the kitchen as if he was cataloging everything in the room against some internal image. He'd clearly done some research before coming.

"You run the kitchen?" The tall blonde asked.

Well at least she wasn't going to have to look up the translation of Klaus' comment.

"No, but I guess Chef Klaus needs someone to order around. Let's get moving; he doesn't like delays. *Nicht hier!*" She tried to imitate his gruff tone. It actually earned her a laugh.

She had their names by the time she'd shown them where the spices were, though she had to think to remember that the fresh ginger would be in with the other root vegetables.

Trevor, Mister Soccer, was indeed following Kimberlee around.

Kimberlee didn't seem to notice, though it seemed obvious. She was also head of the Debate Club that had just taken down Georgetown University's freshman debate team.

The quiet blonde was Valentina—"But call her Val," Kimberlee had stuck in. Once Dilya heard her name she remembered all of the details. Val was the daughter of the brigadier general stationed at the French embassy as the Defense Attaché. She was also the valedictorian who was taking every advanced placement class on the planet. Well, not every one, because she wasn't in Dilya's Government Affairs, American History, or Political Science. And if she was taking a language, it wasn't

Russian or Mandarin. Val was a science-and-math nerd's science-and-math nerd.

"Trevor's the best cook," Val said in that soft voice of hers. She looked a bit like Emily Beale, but she didn't sound at all like her. Too gentle.

"Mom runs kitchen at the Hay Adams Hotel. If you'd met my mom, you'd know I couldn't help but learn."

"Sound kinda defensive there, Trev," Kimberlee winked at Dilya. "But because Val's French, we made her be the president of the Chef's Club."

"The Chef's Club?" Dilya let her guard down for a moment. Miss Watson wanted her to spend the day going to school with a Chef's Club? She didn't even know that her high school had a such a thing.

"Yeah, the four of us are the whole club, unless you want to join?" Mr. Observant Jimmy made it a little funny. He was the misfit in this group of misfits.

"Ha!" Dilya figured that response would cover a lot of ground. Joining wasn't something she did. Of course she could cook. The chow cooks at the secret Night Stalkers base in Pakistan—where she'd lived after Kee rescued her at age ten—had been her source of food. As soon as she'd figured that out, she'd made friends with them and in turn they'd taught her to cook—and turned a blind eye whenever she secreted away a bit of dinner in case life went wrong again. She'd eventually managed to observe the food locker combinations and had no longer needed to hide food under her cot.

She'd also watched Emily Beale cook. Often, when there was no mission, Emily would make a special meal for her crew. Dilya had never helped, but she'd watched and done her best to memorize each step.

"King of war games," Kimberlee offered another of her asides, nodding toward Jimmy.

"Not war games. They're strategy games."

"Guns, tanks, spaceships with nuclear weapons?"

"Yeah," Jimmy admitted and tipped his face down just enough for a long chunk of wavy brown hair to slip over his eyes.

"King of the war games," Kimberlee summed up.

Kimberlee might not know the difference, but Dilya certainly did. Her mother was a sniper, the ultimate in *tactical* warfare. And her father was a leading geopolitical global *strategy* consultant to the President and the Joint Chiefs of Staff.

"Why do you cook?"

But Chef Klaus returned from where he'd been called away to consult on a soup before Jimmy could answer her question.

"Today we're going to start with learning how to a sharpen a knife," Chef Klaus did his looming vulture thing over them. "Then if you somehow manage to master that task, I will teach you how to peel ginger."

5

<hr>

An hour later it seemed they were no closer to satisfying him than when they began. Trevor was the closest with Val as a near second—she finally had graduated to a mere sniff of disdain before he blunted her knife's edge on a steel and told her to try again.

"I never knew there was so much to just sharpening a blade," Kimberlee whispered sadly after her latest effort was blunted and returned with an outright scoff.

Then Chef Klaus focused his ire on her. "That's not a weapon of war you're wielding there, Miss Dilya Stevenson. It's a tool of art." And with a single stroke he wiped out twenty minutes of painstaking work. She'd had about enough of this.

"I'm sorry, sir," Dilya glared at him across the table. "My first knife was a KA-BAR 11-7/8" knife. But I was only ten and the leather-wrapped handle was too big for my hand. So my mother bought me a Cold Steel Recon 11-3/4" Tanto point with a black DLC coating over a VG-1 stainless blade. *That* is what I learned to sharpen."

Klaus stared down his long nose at her.

"*Es ist hier?*"

"*Jawohl.*" She'd heard Val use that as a strong affirmative.

With a tip of his head, he sent her to fetch it. On her return, she considered doing many things, but common sense had prevailed and she handed it, still in its sheath, across the steel table where they sat lined up on their stools. The members of the Chef's Club didn't even pretend to be sharpening their knives, instead watching her avidly. She tried to ignore it, but wasn't having much luck.

Chef Klaus tugged the knife free—on his third try. It required a strong pull and it was easier if the sheath was strapped to a body part. When he glared at her, she was careful to show nothing.

After inspecting the blade carefully, he stepped to the cutting board and dragged it lightly across one of the overripe tomatoes they'd been trying to slice. It slid through the loose skin without a wrinkle and created a slice so clean that the tomato might have still been fresh and firm.

He wiped it carefully with a cloth, replaced it in the sheath and returned it to her. She made a show of strapping it onto her thigh over her jeans. It wasn't the sort of thing to be left lying about. She had a small combination knife safe in her room. The Secret Service had made her leave her sidearm at her parents' house.

"Do you know how to use that blade?"

"I've been trained by my mother," Dilya offered him her best smile. "But I haven't had a reason to use it…yet."

"I could almost like you, Miss Stevenson," Chef Klaus condescended before waving for them to return to their sharpening.

"Super cool," Jimmy whispered.

Which might be the first compliment she'd ever received from a classmate in the two years she'd been in the States and going to a real school.

"You really know how to use that?" Trevor asked as he once again began working his blade in a swirl of vegetable oil on the slab of black sharpening stone. It didn't sound like he doubted her, more like she'd surprised him.

"Her mom is a sniper on the Hostage Rescue Team," Val answered for her.

Dilya could only blink at her. She'd thought she was invisible at school—as invisible as was possible in such a group of DC's overachiever kids. School hadn't mattered to her, but it had been important to Kee and Archie, so she worked hard to get her A's…and to *not* be noticed.

"Oh, man," Jimmy groaned. "That isn't super cool, that's super wicked extra cool."

"If you think my mom is cool," Dilya couldn't help being pleased. Kee was an awesome mom. "You should have met her commanding officer before she retired. She was the first woman to fly helicopters for the Night Stalkers."

Dilya didn't know if they'd ever let her do that, but if they did, that was her dream. A sniper like Kee or a pilot like Emily. That would indeed be super wicked extra cool.

6

They'd eventually graduated from knife sharpening to ginger peeling—by the end of which Jimmy was wearing a pair of bright blue Band-Aids. The lunch was a rich borscht and corned beef on rye sandwiches, big enough to satisfy even Trevor, served right there at the counter with the other chefs.

That was a welcome respite. All morning they had kept asking her questions—about her and about the White House. While it would be rude not to answer, she wished she'd managed to slip in more questions of her own. Except she wasn't used to speaking. She was used to listening. By the time she'd think up her own question, someone would already be talking again.

At least over lunch they started asking questions of the sous chefs instead.

Finally able to listen, Dilya realized that the Chef's Club had been doing this for a while. They'd ask to meet some elite chef—there were a lot of those in DC—and they'd go get a free class.

"I know the chefs at Pauley's Island. Would that help?"

"We didn't even dare try there." "Wow, really?"

One of the chefs was amused that the group had braved asking the White House for a visit, but not Pauley's.

"One of my mom's closest friend's family owns it." Actually, Tim was also one of her friends. He'd been there at the 5D's base since the very first day—doing his best to make her laugh when everything had been so different and terrifying. "I'm sure Tim Maloney would be glad to set it up. Wait, I don't know where he's stationed. I guess I could call his mom."

"That does it," Kimberlee declared.

"It absolutely does," Trevor agreed.

"Madame President?" Jimmy turned to Val.

Val thumped her soup spoon on the counter like a gavel with a bright ting, "You are hereby inducted as an official member of the Chef's Club. All in favor?"

The others all said, "Aye!"

"The ayes have it. Welcome, Dilya Stevenson."

Dilya didn't know what to do with that. She'd never belonged to anything. But she couldn't figure how to get out of it without hurting their feelings.

That question plagued her through lessons on: measuring flour (by weight, never by volume), grating ginger (never mincing), mincing crystallized ginger (never grating), sampling a dozen different sugars, and tasting butter (salted, unsalted, organic, English

Midlands, and finally French butter from Brittany). They spent the whole afternoon on ingredients. There were only thirteen ingredients in gingerbread, including all the spices and everything, but they spent a long time learning about each one.

Did Emily Beale know all this? Dilya made a bet with herself that she did. So she paid extra attention and made sure to ask about anything that was unclear, even if it meant interrupting someone.

"Tomorrow, we will mix and bake," Chef Klaus announced. "If you learn very fast, we will decorate as well. Now go away. Get out of my kitchen, *Kinder*. I have a dinner that must be served to people far more important than you."

"I hate being called a child," Val whispered once they were well clear of the kitchen.

Dilya agreed completely. She also wasn't quite ready to see everyone go. She was unsure why, but she'd learned to trust her instincts—or at least the ones that told her when to hide or run. Maybe she'd listen to this one too.

"You know, just down this hall, the White House has a Chocolate Shop. The chef is my friend." There was that word again. She'd always applied it to friendly adults: the former and current President, the Chief of Staff, chefs, pilots, gunners.

If they were friends, then what was she supposed to call the Chef's Club's members? What was their agenda for "inducting" her? Just to get into Pauley's? No, she'd already made the offer before they did that.

She'd always loved the amazing scents of the

Chocolate Shop, almost as much as the treats themselves. Chef Clive Andrews teased her with funny looks about her silence. As if she'd ever known what to say. If the others noticed, they were too excited to comment on it as the chef explained the tempering of chocolate and pulled out a tray of holiday truffles he was developing.

She was no wiser by the time she escorted them back to the East Wing entrance.

7

"**A**re you my friend?"

Emily tried to make sense of the question. Was the problem the question or because it was four in the morning?

"Who is this?"

"It's me, Dilya." Then there was a small gasp. "I'm so sorry. I forgot about the time zones. How far away is Montana?"

"Three thousand…" No. "Two hours. I think." She'd know for sure if she could wake up.

"I'm sorry. I'll go away and—"

"Wait! Just hang on, Dilya." She took her phone into the bathroom and shut the door. She'd accidentally left the ringer on and, thankfully, it seemed as if Mark had slept through it. "Now what was your question?" She sat on the edge of the tub, then stood to throw a towel over it before she sat back down. She pulled another one over her bare legs. It was only a little damp.

"It's stupid."

"Good. Because if it was a smart question, I wouldn't be able to answer it right now."

Dilya remained silent. Emily tried to remember the last time she'd received a call from the girl, and wasn't sure she ever had.

"You asked if I was your friend?"

"Yes," her voice was tiny.

"Well, you aren't my daughter, so I guess that's about the best word for it. Yes, I'm your friend." She had her own issues with that, but this call wasn't about her, so she shut them out. "Don't you want to be?"

"No. Yes. I… Oh pooh!"

Emily had to fight hard not to laugh. Winnie-the-Pooh was the first book Dilya had learned English from and Pooh's typical curse had stuck with Dilya ever since. Emily also remembered that odd negatives still tripped Dilya up sometimes.

"Do you want to be my friend?"

"Yes. I—" Dilya sighed. "I bet I'd make more sense if I'd slept last night. Is a kid supposed to have adults for friends?"

"Sure, why not? Besides, you aren't really a kid anymore." Especially not with the things she'd survived.

"But if adults are my friends, then what do I call people my age?"

"Hasn't this ever come up before?"

"No!" Dilya practically shouted. "My friends are Tim and Big John. They're White House chefs and the heads of Secret Service details. Don't know how to have friends!" Then she seemed to manage a breath. "I guess… Like at school and stuff."

Emily hung her head and tried not to think about the parallels in her own life. Friends were a new concept to her as well.

"I—" she started then stopped again. "I've always just had a team. Or at least for a long time that's all I had. I flew with your mom and dad, Connie, Lola, and all the others."

"But you're *Emily Beale,*" Dilya protested.

Emily sat up and narrowed her eyes, until she saw herself in the bathroom mirror wearing a faded West Point t-shirt and a slightly damp bath towel. She closed her eyes again.

"What do you mean?"

Dilya sputtered in surprise. "You're…you! Everyone wants to be just like you."

"You want to be just like me?"

"Well, not the blonde and tall part, I've kinda given up on that, but the rest of it, absolutely!"

"Dilya," Emily had had many strange conversations, including the one with Miss Watson yesterday, but this was fast outpacing that. "I'm just a woman. I'm not even a pilot anymore."

"But you're Emily Beale!"

"Stop saying that. Please?"

"Well, okay… But you *totally* are!"

"Dilya."

"Okay. I'm sorry I called. I'm sorry I woke you up."

"I'm not."

Again her voice had gone tiny, "You're not?"

"You get to call me anytime you want. Day or night. I mean it."

"Because my mom was on your team?"

"Because I like you. *You* are my friend."

Dilya actually sniffled. "Okay…thanks." Another sniffle. "Emily?"

"Uh-huh."

"Is it okay if I still want to be like you, even though you're my friend?"

"How about you being more like *you?*" That definitely echoed some pieces of what Miss Watson had told her.

"I don't know. It's kind of…I guess…lonely being me."

"You'll find friends your own age, Dilya. It doesn't mean that the grownups are going to be any less your friends."

"Kinda like a team? Everyone always wanted to be on your team."

"Teams are different than friends."

"How?"

"It's four in the morning, Dilya. Give me a break." She'd forgotten about Dilya's insatiable appetite for answers. She always wanted to know.

"Okay," Emily tried to clear her head. "You lead a team. You have responsibilities for their actions, if not their lives. But you get to be yourself with friends."

There was a long pause before Dilya responded, "I like that explanation."

"I do to," she just hoped that she remembered it when she woke up.

"Thanks. I'm…no longer sorry I called."

"Anytime. Seriously," though she had to fight to keep a massive yawn silent.

"Emily?"

"Uh-huh?"

"I love you, Emily."

"Love you too, Dilya." The end-of-call tone came so fast, she wasn't sure Dilya had heard her answer. As far as she knew, Dilya had never told anyone except her new parents that she loved them.

The innocence of a child's love. Except Dilya was no child. She was a young woman who had seen an even worse slice of the world than Emily had. And if Miss Watson was right, she understood exactly what was happening to her in a way that Emily never had.

When she crawled back into bed, she didn't care if Mark was asleep, she just curled up against him. Without questions, he held her as she cried on his shoulder.

When she was done, she whispered to him softly, "I love you, Mark."

In answer, he just kept holding her tight. It was all she needed.

8

Dilya had the kitchen set up, even before Chef Klaus came in. She had each of the ingredients aligned in an arc, including the ones they'd spent so much time preparing yesterday. She even prepared the cookie sheets with parchment paper—better for crispy edges and bottoms than silicone mats he'd told them. She tore off the correct lengths and tacked them in place with quick swipes of butter underneath the corners.

Chef Klaus looked surprised for only an instant when he came in.

He neatened the rows to make everything perfectly linear, orderly and symmetrical. She let him. As soon as he was done and had gone to hang up his coat, she moved everything back to the arc it had been. It would be easier to reach everything, radially from one position, the way she'd arranged it.

He stepped back into the main kitchen and stuttered to a halt just as the others arrived.

Without speaking, she simply reached out her hands to touch each item without moving from where she stood, rather than having them spread neatly down the length of the table.

The chef made a show of buttoning up his white chef's coat and pulling on his towering hat before he offered her a nod. He even made a grimace that just might have been a smile.

Through the morning they made numerous batches of dough. The variations to make hard sheets of gingerbread and soft ginger cookies. The difference between over- and under-beaten. Proper aeration of the mixture. Why different ingredients were added at different times. That was when quiet Val finally stepped into her own. She and the chef discussed baking soda activation, protein molecule deformation in the eggs, ingredient density, different mixing techniques to ensure even distribution of the grated versus the minced ginger…

Even Kimberlee's eyes were crossing by the time they were done with Val's questions. And Dilya suspected that it only stopped because Val finally realized how thoroughly she'd monopolized the chef. She wasn't a team leader the way Emily was—charging to the front and proving who was best, while beckoning others to try to follow. Val was simply one of the Chef's Club with her own interests and specialties.

Maybe these people didn't need a leader.

Maybe they were just friends.

She toyed with that idea through the rest of the day. They'd rolled out the dough perfectly evenly—done by placing thick rubber bands on either end of the rolling pins so that every spot of dough was exactly the same thickness.

"What should we make?"

A gingerbread house was out of the question. They'd all seen the framework of the massive traditional Christmas gingerbread White House taking shape in Clive's kitchen yesterday afternoon.

"Is there a game that the President likes to play? Maybe we could make a gingerbread version of it for the First Family." Jimmy was clearly picturing ray guns and spaceships.

"Yes there is." First Lady Anne Darlington-Thomas stepped into the kitchen. "My husband likes to think he can do *The New York Times* Sunday crossword. Which means every week my Sunday breakfast is about telling him the answers. *Two across. A seven-letter word for a fool.* Easy: *husband.* As in one who thinks he's doing the crossword on his own. I'm so glad that's now done for the week." Though her easy smile said she might enjoy the weekly ritual just as much as the President.

All the kids of the Chef's Club laughed despite their obvious awe at being in the First Lady's presence.

"Good morning, Dilya."

"Hi, Anne." The others looked at her goggle-eyed.

"Are you all having fun?"

There were a lot of mumbled, "Yes ma'am."

"Well, if Chef Klaus gets out of line, just sic Dilya on him. If anyone can keep Herman in line, she's the one. Now I have to go face him about the menu for next week's Residence reception for the Australian Prime Minister." And she breezed off into the back of the kitchen.

"Whoa!" Kimberlee whispered.

"Why did you use her first name?" Even Trevor was whispering.

"She asked me to. Besides, I'm nanny for her kid most days after school."

They all exchanged looks, but it was Jimmy who voiced the group's consensus opinion. "Super wicked uber-cool."

ilya's face and sides hurt.

She'd didn't get why, until Val made one of her dry French observations or Kimberlee teased Trevor.

Laughing and smiling. She simply wasn't used to doing that for a whole afternoon.

With Kimberlee, as head of Debate Club, leading the way, they'd mapped out a gingerbread crossword puzzle. *Christmas* down the middle; the First Family's names attached crosswise (though they had to use the First Daughter's middle name to make it all work—she actually had two of them, so she got to be in twice). Then they'd toyed with words until it was totally filled.

Chef Klaus had taught them piping and flooding techniques—requiring different mixes of royal icing because one had to stay where it was placed and the other had to flow to fill in the squares that needed to be white. Jimmy tackled the vast expanse of cookie that needed conversion into the puzzle. He was in nerd heaven.

Val had the best handwriting with a piping bag, so she took a large sheet of dark gingerbread and began writing humorous clues on it.

Dilya sat with Kimberlee and Trevor calling out suggestions for Val and making ornate letters on round, softer ginger cookies.

Whenever a cookie was broken or had its icing smeared past recovery, it was shared around, until they were all sick of them—even with tall glasses of milk. Kimberlee scrounged up a brown paper bag and started filling it with the broken bits and pieces.

All through the long afternoon, they sat together and worked on the ginger crossword. And all afternoon, Dilya could only sit in wonder. At school lunchtime, Kimberlee's table was always popular. Trevor sometimes sat with her and sometimes with his teammates. Val sat with a few other equally brilliant friends. She wasn't sure where Jimmy ate lunch.

Dilya ate with no one. Half the time, she didn't even go into the cafeteria, preferring to find a quiet corner. For this one great day though, her afternoon was filled with laughter and ideas.

As the day progressed, it became clearer and clearer where the members of the Chef's Club would end up.

Val was headed straight for the diplomatic corps— that was so obvious. She was too smart and too nice to do anything else. Maybe a science liaison or something.

Kimberlee could well follow in her senator-father's

footsteps. Maybe she'd even end up in the White House someday.

Trevor was going to cook—it was clear that he was in the club for a lot more reasons than following around after Kimberlee. Dilya did wonder how long it was going to take him to ask her out. Kimberlee was going to be in for a big surprise, as she really was clueless that Trevor was hot for her.

And even in joking, she could sense Jimmy's clear grasp of how strategy worked. He could teach her some things about that, but he was weak in the real world. They'd have to talk about his strategy skills and what was actually going on globally—instead of inside some online game.

And she…was totally fooling herself. Why would they want her around? To get into Pauley's Island restaurant and the White House Chocolate Shop. To have a story to tell in the cafeteria.

She wouldn't fit in at any of their lunch tables. Everything they'd built this weekend was just about this weekend. Dilya wasn't dumb enough to believe there was a future here. She'd enjoy the day, but that would be the end of it.

They finished the giant crossword, scooting it onto a big silver platter she found in the butler's pantry. A shallow silver bowl with FDR's family crest stamped into the side was filled with the lettered cookies while Val wrote "A First Family Christmas" across the top of the puzzle. In the bottom corner, she wrote "Thanks for having us." Below that they each signed their names with piped royal icing.

Dilya looked at the five names together. For a weekend they'd come together just like one of Emily's teams. She liked that. It gave her ideas for the future. Someday she'd have a team. More importantly, someday she'd have friends. Maybe like these.

It was hard leaving the kitchen. Chef Klaus actually did smile when he saw the finished project. He promised to make sure it was delivered this evening with after-dinner tea. He came around and shook each person's hand and gave them a personalized signed copy of his White House cookbook. Dilya peeked at her own, it simply said, *"Niemals aufhören!"* Thankfully, beneath that he'd written, "Don't stop!" As if.

When they neared the exit, Kimberlee slipped a brown paper bag to her. Dilya peeked inside; it contained all of the failed and broken cookies.

"I'm too nervous to try and smuggle it out through security. But you can do it. Everyone likes you."

Dilya looked down at the bag and back at Kimberlee. "I don't understand."

"They taste awesome. We can't let these go to waste. You smuggle them out of the White House tomorrow and we can share them during lunch."

Then with a wave, they were all gone.

Dilya stood inside the East Wing entrance as she weighed the cookies in her hand. There would be plenty to share at a lunch. It was silly, it was just a place to sit. A place to sit…with people. With *friends!* And she could feel the smile tug at her cheeks once more.

As she walked back through the White House, she looked upon the shining winter wonderland of plastic icicles dripping from high ceilings and fake snow sweeping under brightly lit Christmas trees.

Emily was right. There were teams and there were friends. And she'd make sure that her life was filled with both of them.

BE sure not to miss the companion story: Emily's Christmas Gift, a Henderson's Ranch story.

EMILY'S CHRISTMAS GIFT
(EXCERPT)

IF YOU LIKED THIS, YOU'LL LOVE THE COMPANION STORY.

M. L.
BUCHMAN
3-TIME BOOKLIST TOP 10 ROMANCE AUTHOR OF THE YEAR
EMILY'S
CHRISTMAS
GIFT
A HENDERSON'S RANCH BIG SKY STORY

*E*mily watched Mark being as calm as could be and tried not to resent it. When the heavy Montana snowstorms of December kept them indoors at the main ranch house, he was content to slouch low on the couch and watch a Disney movie with the girls in the cozy family area off the kitchen.

If they wanted to build a fort—Emily always thought of it as a fort, though the girls kept insisting they were tents—Mark would reconfigure the family sitting area off the kitchen no matter what inconvenience it caused the adults.

Between the three of them, they made sure that each construction looked unlike any prior effort. A tropical paradise one time, decorated mostly with one of the ranch hand's awful Hawaiian shirt collection. Another time, a Cheyenne teepee built with Mark's mother's lovely weavings. She'd particularly liked that one. Being in Montana, and especially if Julie was around to help, Western themes were common, often with horse tack or some of her rodeo trophies for decoration.

In the summers Mark lived to fly tourists around in his helicopter and fish, but in the winter his one joy was keeping his girls happy.

That she herself was one of "his girls" always made their daughters giggle with delight. And she *was* happy. All she had to do was watch her daughters and she let their constantly bubbling joy wash over her. They might build their forts—*tents* with their father. But it was never considered complete until she had joined them for the final tour. Mark often left some final task for her to do so that she'd at least feel included. Then they would all lie in it together—Mark at the center with all three of "his girls" clinging happily to him.

Those were the best moments of her life. Perhaps a close second to waking in his arms on the long quiet winter mornings before Tessa and Belle sprang to life like a pair of Jill-in-the-boxes.

She'd known he was a good man and a great commander, but his daughters had never met "The Viper" who used to scare the shit out of everybody, including her. His steel gray eyes had rarely been revealed from behind his mirrored shades. He'd even proposed to her while wearing them—after dark. Which was perhaps the only thing that had kept her from turning into a complete empty-headed mush in that moment.

But his daughters only saw the sky gray that his eyes shone when he was happiest—and the mirrored shades were now worn only in the strong Montana sun. It was impossible for her *not* be happy while she watched the stern, taciturn, demanding Major Mark "The Viper" Henderson (retired) have no compunction about acting as the total goofball with his girls. He was a better father than she was a mother, but she didn't know what to do about that. When they were upset, it was her they came to, so she still had something. But it often meant she got the tears and Mark earned all the cheers.

Emily didn't resent it…much. She mostly just wished it was somehow different.

She turned to the fire and watched what she could see of the flames. They were partially blocked by a great bulge in this week's fort, which was huge by any previous standard.

This room was where the family lived during the day when they weren't out on the ranch. The high-timbered main room and the dining room with its forty-person pine table was for the guests. In the long, bitter, off-season months, it was also where all the locals gathered for the occasional party to break the monotony of winter.

That was for others. The family lived in the kitchen. The kitchen itself was a full commercial setup, decorated like in ranch-house warm timber and cool granite stone. At the near end stood a large plank table of Douglas fir where the family and the ranch hands ate their meals together.

This sitting area to the side had a big stone fireplace, and a scattering of couches and armchairs enough for the entire staff…or there had been until the kids started showing up. Once they graduated from lap-sized, they would have to squeeze in some more furniture. The bookcases that lined the river stone walls already had more shelves added to accommodate the girls' picture books.

Of course more furniture couldn't happen with their latest fort in place—she could only see half the fire from her favorite end of the couch.

It was like a mighty Christmas igloo, its walls built high with pillows raided from all of the guest cabins that were closed for the winter. Mark had waded out into the freezing dawn this morning to cut down and drag home a ten-foot larch to stand at its center. Now, with the tree up and their pillow-wall built, the three of them were madly working away inside. Only the tree's single uppermost branch was visible above the domed roof, like a wide smoke hole escaping the dome of pillows.

Whenever there was a newborn about, either Chelsea's or Julie's boy, their father was instantly abandoned without further thought—which made her feel a little better. Of course, then Emily had to keep a close eye so that the girls didn't smother the two infants with affection. How in the world she'd raised two such…*girls* was a mystery to her. At five, Tessa was an utter extrovert who had all the ranch hands completely wrapped around her tiny pinkie. Belle at three was the steadier one, but only by comparison.

Emily didn't pace when the heavy snow and the biting cold winds forced them to remain indoors, but she wished she'd taken up watching sports on television or something. But after a career of flying helicopters first to war and then to wildfire, watching a bunch of guys chase a football up and down a chunk of AstroTurf in little one- and two-yard spurts couldn't be called exciting.

"I'm absolutely hiring Mark for the next seventeen years," Chelsea plummeted down into the big armchair beside Emily's end of the couch, then had to drag her fingers through her long hair to toss it over her shoulder so she could see. Her cheeks were brilliant red after crossing the snow from where she and her husband, the ranch manager, lived on the other side of the barnyard. Maybe Emily should grow her gold-blonde hair as long, the way Mark kept hinting, but it had been chopped dead straight to her shoulders for her entire life.

Emily saw Mark now sitting on the braided rug with Chelsea's three-month old boy Christopher cradled in his arms—whose hair was already as red as his mother's. Tessa and Belle were leaning on his thighs from either side and reaching over to inspect the infant who watched with such wide, serious eyes. Her own fair hair hadn't been passed on to either daughter, having no chance against Mark's genes from his brown-haired father and Cheyenne mother.

"Or maybe I'll just knock you off and get two husbands, keep Doug for me and have Mark for the kid." Chelsea extended her feet toward the fire.

"I'm notoriously hard to kill." Emily's specialty had been black-in-black missions. Black ops so sensitive that they were talked about with no one, ever. And so dangerous that each one was a curse of its own. Mark accompanied her on or referred vaguely to four—she'd stopped counting as she neared ten.

"Oh, don't worry, Emily," Chelsea slouched lower. "I'd like, uh, get Julie to do it for me. She was raised a cowgirl and knows how to do the icky stuff."

"I'm a horsegirl now. And do what?" Julie settled very slowly on the couch beside Emily, careful not to wake Jared asleep in her arms. Like her own children, Jared had his father's dark hair and eyes rather than Julia's wheat blonde and blue. If he'd slept through the snowy trek down the hill from their cabin, then it would take far more than a small bump to wake him, but Emily knew better than to say such a thing to a new mother. She had to smile at her own worries about Tessa in the beginning.

She did scoop up Jared and hold him while Julie shed her thick coat and tossed it over a maple wood chair. Then she settled back on the plaid sofa and took Jared back, again with infinite care.

Like the toddler-magnets they were, Tessa and Belle appeared on either side of Julie. Tessa sat on Julie's far side, but Belle pushed and squirmed—with plenty of bumps that Jared never noticed—until she was sitting between Emily and Julie. Emily looped an arm around her daughter, not as if there was anywhere else to put it, and kissed her on top of the head.

"I need you to…uh," Chelsea glanced at the two young girls before answering Julie, "…*remove* Emily for me. Kinda permanently so I can have Mark as a full-time babysitter."

"Too late," Julie gently blocked Belle reaching over

to wake Jared. Belle was completely enamored of Jared's big eyes and the two of them could stare at each other for hours. "I've already got dibs. Besides, I thought we liked Emily?"

"We do. But where has that gotten us?"

Keep reading at fine retailers everywhere

ABOUT THE AUTHOR

M.L. Buchman started the first of over 50 novels and even more short stories while flying from South Korea to ride across the Australian Outback. All part of a solo around-the-world bicycle trip (a mid-life crisis on wheels) that ultimately launched his writing career.

Booklist has selected his military and firefighter series(es) as 3-time "Top 10 Romance of the Year." NPR and Barnes & Noble have named other titles "Top 5 Romance of the Year." In 2016 he was a finalist for RWA's RITA award.

He has flown and jumped out of airplanes, can single-hand a fifty-foot sailboat, and has designed and built two houses. In between writing, he also quilts. M.L. is constantly amazed at what can be done with a degree in geophysics. He also writes: contemporary romance, thrillers, and SF. More info at: www.mlbuchman.com

Join the conversation:
www.mlbuchman.com

Other works by M. L. Buchman:

The Night Stalkers

MAIN FLIGHT
The Night Is Mine
I Own the Dawn
Wait Until Dark
Take Over at Midnight
Light Up the Night
Bring On the Dusk
By Break of Day

WHITE HOUSE HOLIDAY
Daniel's Christmas
Frank's Independence Day
Peter's Christmas
Zachary's Christmas
Roy's Independence Day
Damien's Christmas

AND THE NAVY
Christmas at Steel Beach
Christmas at Peleliu Cove

5E
Target of the Heart
Target Lock on Love
Target of Mine

Firehawks

MAIN FLIGHT
Pure Heat
Full Blaze
Hot Point
Flash of Fire
Wild Fire

SMOKEJUMPERS
Wildfire at Dawn
Wildfire at Larch Creek
Wildfire on the Skagit

Delta Force

Target Engaged
Heart Strike
Wild Justice

White House Protection Force

Off the Leash
On Your Mark
In the Weeds

Where Dreams

Where Dreams are Born
Where Dreams Reside
Where Dreams Are of Christmas
Where Dreams Unfold
Where Dreams Are Written

Eagle Cove

Return to Eagle Cove
Recipe for Eagle Cove
Longing for Eagle Cove
Keepsake for Eagle Cove

Henderson's Ranch

Nathan's Big Sky
Big Sky, Loyal Heart

Love Abroad

Heart of the Cotswolds: England
Path of Love: Cinque Terre, Italy

Dead Chef Thrillers

Swap Out!
One Chef!
Two Chef!

Deities Anonymous

Cookbook from Hell: Reheated
Saviors 101

SF/F Titles

The Nara Reaction
Monk's Maze
the Me and Elsie Chronicles

Strategies for Success (NF)

Managing Your Inner Artist/Writer
Estate Planning for Authors

SIGN UP FOR M. L. BUCHMAN'S
NEWSLETTER TODAY

and receive:
Release News
Free Short Stories
a Free Book

Do it today. Do it now.
http://free-book.mlbuchman.com

www.ingramcontent.com/pod-product-compliance
Lightning Source LLC
Chambersburg PA
CBHW032051180726
48284CB00004B/1293